MARTHA
THE MOVIE MOUSE

STORY AND PICTURES
BY ARNOLD LOBEL

HarperTrophy
A Division of HarperCollins*Publishers*

LC Number: 66-18654
ISBN 0-06-023970-0 (lib. bdg.)
ISBN 0-06-443318-8 (pbk.)

First Harper Trophy edition, 1993.

for Belia

and Ursula

and Dim Dim

In a dirty part of town
Martha watched the rain come down.
"What I need and right away,"
Said Martha, "is a place to stay.
My luck's been bad, but I would give
My whiskers for a place to live.

"I've stayed in houses," Martha said,
"And it's a wonder I'm not dead.
I found behind each kitchen door
A waiting mousetrap on the floor,
And children in those people places
Popped guns at me in battle chases."
Cried Martha, "I am in despair.
I can't find friendship anywhere."

Martha wandered every street.
She had no home, just tired feet.
The driving rain changed into snow
As colder winds began to blow.
But then, against the icy night,

She saw a very pleasant sight:
A movie theater, lights aglow.
Said Martha, "Here, for all I know,
Is just the place I'm looking for.
I'll go right in and I'll explore."

Martha quickly ran inside
And there she opened both eyes wide.
Underneath a chandelier
The lobby gleamed with warmth and cheer.
A candy counter stood nearby
Piled with goodies, bright and high.
Cracker Jacks and chocolate bars,
Nuts and bubble-gum cigars.

Martha wandered every street.
She had no home, just tired feet.
The driving rain changed into snow
As colder winds began to blow.
But then, against the icy night,

She saw a very pleasant sight:
A movie theater, lights aglow.
Said Martha, "Here, for all I know,
Is just the place I'm looking for.
I'll go right in and I'll explore."

Martha quickly ran inside
And there she opened both eyes wide.
Underneath a chandelier
The lobby gleamed with warmth and cheer.
A candy counter stood nearby
Piled with goodies, bright and high.
Cracker Jacks and chocolate bars,
Nuts and bubble-gum cigars.

Behind a large soft-drink machine
Martha fell asleep, serene.

The next day, after sleeping late,
Said Martha, "I'll investigate
This building, for it really seems
I've found the mouseplace of my dreams."
She climbed some stairs and met a man.
"Hello," he said. "My name is Dan."
"Hello," said Martha. "You seem nice."
"I am," said Dan. "I'm fond of mice.
I work alone, as you can see.
Please stay and keep me company.

"Each day I come to do my job.
I push the plug and turn the knob
To start this large and fine machine
That flickers pictures on a screen.
The film goes in and round about
And movies are projected out."
Then Martha said, "I do regret
I haven't seen a movie yet."

Martha jumped up on a chair.
She found a peephole, small and square,
Through which she saw to her surprise
A dark room of enormous size
Where people sat, row after row,
And watched the motion-picture show.

While outside there was snow and sleet,
Inside the theater life was sweet.
For Martha watched with great delight
A double feature every night.
She dined three times a day or more
On popcorn from the theater floor.

Her heart was gay. She cried with bliss,
"No mouse has ever lived like this!"
In wonder Martha watched the screen.
She saw things she had never seen.
Indians with painted faces
Fought cowboys in great desert spaces.

And pirates sailed through crashing waves
To islands filled with treasure caves.

Policemen chased big gangster cars....

Strange monsters came from planet Mars.

One evening Martha sat entranced
And watched some girls who sang and danced.
The music had a jazzy beat
So Martha tapped her little feet.
She listened to the catchy song
And then began to sing along.
Although her tone was mousy thin,
She raised her voice and joined right in.

But Martha's joy did not last long,
For sadly something went quite wrong.
A lady hearing Martha's squeak
Jumped up and loudly shouted, "EEEK!"
Then great commotion filled the hall
And Martha knew she'd caused it all.
"Help! Help! A mouse!" more ladies cried
As Martha ran out, terrified.

"It seems," said Martha, "very clear,
These people do not want me here."
Though Dan tried hard to make her stay,
She shook her head and went away.
Dan said, "I hate to see you go.
We'll always be good friends, you know."

And Martha, homeless as before,
Slept under garbage cans once more.
She dreamed of movies each long night,
In color and in black and white.

All winter, in a freezing sewer
Where things to eat grew scarce and fewer,
Cold Martha sat, just getting thinner.
She had no lunch and seldom dinner.

She cried, "I'm hungry!" and she ran
Back through the snowy streets to Dan.
She ran and did not stop until
She found a theater windowsill.
"I've searched for you and I've been worried,"
Said Dan, who very quickly hurried
To bring her in and cover her.
He wiped the snowflakes off her fur.

That evening while they ate and drank
They heard a noise . . . a crash . . . a clank.
Dan turned quite pale and cried with fear,
"My film projector's slipped a gear!
It's caused a very bad short circuit.
The thing is broken; I can't work it!
There's only one thing I can do.
I'll start projector number two.

"I love you, Martha," Dan said later.
"You're super! There is no one greater.
From me, here is a rose bouquet.
Your songs and dances saved the day."
Said Martha, "It was all for you.
I knew somehow I'd muddle through."

AMAZING MOUSE! the headlines read.
All over town the news was spread.

"But that," said Dan with great dismay,
"Will cause a very long delay.
When people see the screen is black,
They all will want their money back."
Dan trembled there; he mopped his brow.
But Martha said, "I'll help you now.
Just light the stage with spotlights, Dan,
And I will carry out my plan."

She rushed downstairs into the room
Where all the people sat in gloom.
They grumbled, "We would like to know
What happened to the picture show."
As Martha jumped across the stage
A gentleman cried out in rage,
"We thought this was a movie house.
We did not come to see a mouse!"

Martha stood high on her toes.
She twirled her tail and twitched her nose.
She took a breath and with a smile
Began to dance with grace and style.

Remembering the things she'd seen
Not long ago upon the screen,
She danced the cancan and the tango,
The tarantella and fandango.

Martha pranced a gay gavotte,
Then slid into a slow fox-trot.
She waltzed with many spins and swirls,
Just like those pretty movie girls.

The audience could not resist
As Martha danced a lively twist.
And when she did the bunny hop,
They cried, "Bravo! Please do not stop!"

But Martha
Twirled her tail again.
She sat down on the stage
And then,
Quite softly,
With a voice appealing
Began to sing
With heart and feeling.
She sang
A very long lament
Of garbage dumps
And cold cement.
She sang
About her sad life past,
Of alley cats
She ran from fast.
She sang of mousetraps
Tightly set
And city streets
All dark and wet.
She sang the blues,
A haunting tune
So beautiful
That very soon
The people
Were all moved to tears.
They clapped their hands
And shouted cheers.
That theater
Rocked with celebration
As Martha
Bowed to their ovation.

By bus and train, from near and far
They came to see the famous star.
And Martha's name in flashing lights
Brightened up the darkest nights.

Though Martha
Did enjoy her fame,
Her greatest pleasure
Always came
While watching movies
In her seat,
With lots of popcorn
There to eat.
She sipped a lemon Coke
With ice
And was the happiest of mice.